AFTER SCHOOL

Tap Dancing

Susan Hebach

HIGH
interest
books

Children's Press
A Division of Scholastic Inc.
New York • Toronto • London • Auckland • Sydney

Thanks to the Broadway Bound Dance Academy, Media, PA

Book Design: Michelle Innes
Contributing Editors: Eric Fein, Jennifer Silate

Photo Credits: Cover, pp. 1, 7, 19–20, 23–37 by Maura Boruchow; p. 5 ©
FPG International; p. 9 © Archive Photos; p. 10, 13 © The Everett Collection;
pp. 14, 17, 39 © AP Worldwide Photos

Visit Children's Press on the Internet at:
http://publishing.grolier.com

Library of Congress Cataloging-in-Publication Data

Hebach, Susan.
Tap dancing / by Susan Hebach.
    p. cm. -- (After school)
    Includes bibliographical references (p.) and index.
    ISBN 0-516-23156-1 (lib. bdg.) -- ISBN 0-516-29560-8 (pbk.)
    1. Tap dancing--Juvenile literature. [1. Tap dancing.] I. Title. II. Series.

GV1794 .H43 2001
792.7'8--dc21

                                                          00-065624

CONTENTS

INTRODUCTION

Did you know that tap dance began in the United States more than two hundred years ago? Today, you can find tap dancers all over the world. You can see tap dancers on television, in movies, and on the stage.

Why should you learn to tap dance? To begin with, it is a great way to exercise. You have to be in good physical shape to tap dance well. Concentration also plays an important part in learning tap. You need to focus all your attention on learning the steps. Tap dance helps you understand music, too. When tap dancers put on their tap shoes, they become musicians. Their feet are their musical instruments. Tap teaches you to follow the music so that you can tap along to it. One of the best reasons to take tap is that it's fun. If you are interested in musical theater, it's good to know tap because many musicals have tap dancing in their choreography (arrangement of dance steps).

Gene Kelly was a very famous tap dancer. Here, he performs
in the hit musical *Singin' in the Rain*.

This book takes you inside the world of tap
dance. You will learn the history of tap and
basic tap steps and moves.

CHAPTER ONE

Getting Started

Tap dance is all about making music with your feet. In this way, tap is different from all other kinds of dance. How do tap dancers make music with their feet? They wear special shoes. These shoes have metal taps on the heels and toes. These taps make the sounds you hear. Tap dancers strike the dance floor with their shoes the way drummers hit drums with their sticks.

Taps can make different types of sounds. It all depends on how the tap hits the floor. If the tap hits hard, the sound will be loud. If the tap hits lightly, the sound will be soft. The range of sounds from loud to soft is what gives tap its musical quality.

Learning tap is like learning any other type of dance. All dancers need to learn techniques and foot control. In tap dance, dancers who have good foot control and technique can make

The thick heel on this shoe makes a deep sound.

a wide range of tap sounds. Being in good shape is important. Sometimes tap dancers do steps that are very athletic.

Tap dancers also must learn how to think like musicians. Dancers who understand music are able to choose the tap steps that fit the music they dance to. Some dancers like to choose steps that accent the rhythm of the music. If the music has a lot of drumbeats, a dancer might use steps that are loud and forceful.

TAP DANCE'S BEGINNINGS

Tap dance is a blend of European and African dance styles. English and Irish dances, such as jigs, clogs, and step dances, give tap its basic technique—striking the floor with one's feet. African dances use drumming rhythms, body and arm movements, and improvisation (steps made up on the spot). These African dance elements, together with the European floor sounds, give tap its basic steps and moves.

Tap dance was popular in vaudeville in the first part of the twentieth century (1900–1940). Vaudeville shows were held in theaters. These shows were a series of short comedy skits, songs, and dances. Bill "Bojangles" Robinson, one of the most famous tap dancers, got his start in vaudeville. Tap dance has been popular in movies. Performers such as Fred Astaire and Gene Kelly became stars thanks to their tap dancing skills. They both appeared, together and separately, in dozens of movies.

Bill "Bojangles" Robinson was one of the first African-American movie stars. In 1929, he was the highest-paid African-American performer in the world.

9

9

3Generations

Did You Know?

Since 1989, every May 25th is National Tap Dance Day. The United States Congress chose this date because it was the birthday of legendary tap dancer Bill "Bojangles" Robinson. They felt that it was a good way to honor tap as well as one of its greatest dancers.

of
Tap Legends

The 1989 film *Tap* featured three generations of world-class tap dancers: Sammy Davis, Jr., Gregory Hines, and Savion Glover. *Tap* was Davis's last film. It gave him the chance to show his tap mastery one last time.

By the 1950s, tap was out of fashion. Rock-and-roll music swept the country. New dances, like "The Twist," pushed tap out of the spotlight. It was not until the 1970s that a handful of dancers helped to renew interest in tap. Soon, tap was popular all over again, and this popularity has lasted. Today, tap dance can be seen on television, in film, in dance concerts, and in musical theater.

CHAPTER TWO

Styles of Tap Dance

Rhythm Tap Dance

Rhythm tappers dance mainly to jazz music. Often they tap to different types of music, including Latin, classical, blues, and rap. In rhythm tap, dancers work on creating musical phrases with their taps. The use of improvisation is an important part of rhythm tap. In this way, rhythm tap dancers are like jazz musicians.

Tap Dance and Classical Music

Tap dance is performed to classical music, too. Paul Draper was a well-known tap dancer in the 1940s, 50s, and 60s. He was one of the first dancers to mix tap dance with classical ballet. Leon Collins was another rhythm tap dancer. He choreographed dances to classical pieces, such as *Flight of the Bumble Bee*. Conductor Morton Gould wrote a piece for tap and orchestra to perform together. It was called *The Tap Concerto*. In this musical piece, Gould wrote out the notes and rhythms for the tap dancer to play with his

Paul Draper learned ballet after he learned to tap. Ballet moves helped him to tap dance to classical music.

or her feet. In *The Tap Concerto*, the tap dancer becomes a member of the orchestra.

Musical Theater and Broadway Tap

In a Broadway musical, dance numbers help move the story along. Movements are exaggerated so that people in the back of the theater can see and understand what is happening. Tap dancing in musical productions usually focuses on whole groups, or ensembles, of dancers. When many dancers are on stage at the same time, there is no room for improvisation. Steps and routines are performed precisely by all the dancers.

Spotlight on

Savion Glover

Today's tap dance owes a debt to Savion Glover. He has brought a new generation of fans and dancers to tap, especially men. Glover has done this by using rap and hip-hop to inspire his dancing. He drums the tap floor with his feet. His dancing is rhythmic and energetic, making it exciting to watch. There are times he taps so quickly that his feet are a blur of motion.

Savion Glover created a sensation on Broadway with the success of his show, *Bring in 'Da Noise, Bring in 'Da Funk.* In 1996, he even won a Tony Award for best choreography for *Bring in 'Da Noise, Bring in 'Da Funk.* The show was about tap dance and its history, inspired by today's rap and funk music. Glover's urban and contemporary choreography made the show an instant hit with the public.

Savion Glover performed on Broadway for many years. His first Broadway perfomance was when he was twelve years old, starring in *The Tap Dance Kid.*

CHAPTER THREE

Learning to Tap Dance

SHOES AND DANCE CLOTHES

A good pair of shoes is very important to tap dancers. Sturdy oxfords with taps are the best kinds of shoes for beginners. These shoes provide good balance and good sound. Women who perform tap in chorus dancing sometimes have to wear high-heeled tap shoes. If you are in a musical, the shoes you wear will be determined by your costume.

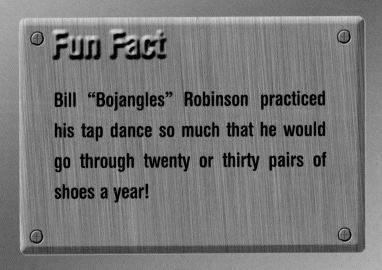

Fun Fact

Bill "Bojangles" Robinson practiced his tap dance so much that he would go through twenty or thirty pairs of shoes a year!

Leotards and tights allow the dancer to move freely.

You need to wear clothes that allow you to move easily when you tap dance. Some tap dance teachers may require that you wear a leotard and tights. Sweatpants and T-shirts also work well for tap. If you wear pants, make sure that they do not cover your shoes. If your pants are too long, you will step on them and muffle the sounds your taps make. Your teacher also needs to see your feet clearly. It's the only way to tell if you are doing the steps properly.

TAP DANCE CLASS

To learn tap, you need to find a good tap dance class. Some high schools may include tap dance as a physical education or after-school activity. Community centers also may offer tap dance classes. For a more serious approach, check out the tap dance schools in your area. You can find dance schools in the Yellow Pages under Dance Instruction. When calling dance schools, tell them your age and ask if they give beginner classes. If they have beginner classes, make sure the class is for your age group. Find out how much classes cost. Look for a studio that has experience teaching tap dance to beginners.

Working with a teacher at least once a week can be a great experience. A teacher can help you learn all the basics. A good teacher helps you improve your skills and reach your goals. Practice is very important. Review the steps that you learn in each class. Once you learn the basics, you can move on to steps that are more difficult.

In tap class, dancers learn their moves and how to work with props, such as canes.

Working with a teacher is not the only reason to go to a dance studio. Studios have floors that are built just for tap dancing. The floors are smooth but not slippery. A dance studio is also a good place to meet people your age. Along with learning to dance, you might even make new friends.

Dancers must warm up their arms and legs before class begins.

A TYPICAL TAP DANCE CLASS

A tap dance class usually is made up of four parts: the warm-up, "across the floor," center combinations and choreography, and improvisation. Here is what happens in each part.

The Warm-up

All dancers start by warming up. The purpose of the warm-up is to get the blood moving through the muscles. In the warm-up, you use many basic tap steps. The warm-up is done to music that has a moderate speed, or tempo.

Across the Floor

After the warm-up, the class often does exercises that go "across the floor." This part of the class focuses on steps that "travel" or move the dancers across the floor. Dancers travel by using a combination of steps. These combinations of steps are designed to help the dancers practice traveling through the dance space. "Across the floor" includes different types of turns, slides, and other steps that require space for "traveling."

Center Combination and Choreography

The next part of the class takes place in the center of the floor. This is where dancers learn new "combinations." A combination is made up of several different basic steps. When these steps are put together, they make a more complex step. Often, many of these combination steps are linked together to create a piece of choreography.

Improvisation

In rhythm tap classes, dancers get the chance to improvise (dance without a set routine) or "jam" at the end of class. Then students can practice what they learned during class. They also get to express their own musical ideas and make up their own steps to the music.

FINDING SOUNDS

Tap shoes have taps on their soles. Each sole has a toe tap and a heel tap. You can make a variety of sounds with these taps. Here are some basic single-sound steps that beginners learn.

Toe Drops and Heel Drops

To do toe drops, stand with your weight evenly spread between both feet. Now lift your toes, keeping your heels on the floor. Next, drop both of your toe taps to the floor. You also can do toe drops with each foot separately, alternating sides.

Toe Drop

Stand with weight
even on both feet.

Lift your toes.

Drop your toes.

Stand on the balls
of your feet.

Drop both heels.

Heel Drop

Or drop one heel at
a time.

To do a heel drop, raise your heels so that you are standing on the balls of your feet. Now drop your heels at the same time. You can do them separately, too, if you like.

Brush

Many of the basic tap steps are done using an action called a brush. A brush is done by

Forward Brush

Strike ground with your foot.
Swing leg forward.

Backward Brush

Strike ground with your foot.
Swing leg backward.

striking the ball of the foot on the floor. You do this as you swing your foot forward or backward. To do a forward brush, swing your foot forward. Strike the floor with your foot so that you make one tap sound. A backward brush is done by swinging your foot back. Again, strike the floor so that a tap sound is made.

Toe Punch

Raise one leg with your toe pointed down.

Strike floor with the edge of toe tap.

Toe Punch

To do a toe punch, stand on one leg. Lift your other foot and point the toe down. Angle your foot so that the edge of the toe tap will hit the floor. Now just hit the edge of the toe tap on the floor to make a deep, low, knocking sound.

Heel Dig

A heel dig is a lot like a toe punch. Stand on one leg with the other foot raised. Now strike the edge of your heel tap on the floor.

Heel Dig

Raise one leg with your toe pointed up.

Strike floor with the edge of heel tap.

BEYOND SINGLE-SOUND STEPS

Here are a few basic steps that build on single-sound steps. They are more difficult, so take your time learning them.

Cramp Roll

A simple cramp roll is a step with four sounds. A cramp roll is made up of these four steps: toe drop, toe drop, heel drop, and heel drop. At the end, both of your feet should be flat on the

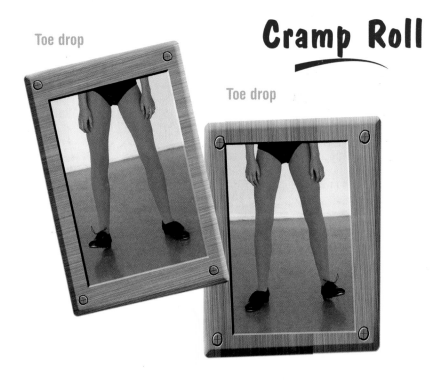

Toe drop

Toe drop

Cramp Roll

Heel drop

Heel drop

End with both feet
flat on the floor.

floor. Try to separate each sound. Make the
sounds equal in length. A cramp roll sounds
like a short drum roll.

Shuffle

A shuffle is a two-sound step that has a forward brush followed by a backward brush. Always brush to the front first. When doing shuffles, make your brush sounds short and clear. Don't let the ball sound drag on the floor when you brush forward or backward. To do a shuffle step, follow the shuffle by putting the same foot on the floor. The shuffle step makes three sounds.

Forward brush

Backward brush

Shuffle

End with both feet flat on the floor.

Ball Change

Lift left foot, shifting weight to your right foot.

Lift right foot, shifting weight to your left foot.

Ball Change

The ball change is a "rocking" step that has two sounds. To do a simple ball change, pick up your right foot. Place the ball of the foot behind you. Now pick up your left foot and put it back down again. You should make one clear sound. Think of this as rocking from back to front.

Put left foot back down.

Shuffle Ball Change

Start with your shuffle and then add a ball change. Make sure you hear four separate sounds when you do it.

Shuffle Ball Change

Forward brush with your right foot.

Backward brush with your right foot.

Shift weight to right foot.

Shift weight to left foot.

Forward brush

Step down on the ball of your foot, stay on your toes.

Flap

Flap

A flap has two sounds. It can travel forward or backward or stay in place. To do walking flaps, brush forward and step down on the ball of your foot. Now do the same with your other foot. You will feel as if you are walking with some added rhythm. Remember to stay on your toes. Try doing the same step moving backward.

Flap Heel

Forward brush

Lift foot

Step down on the ball of your foot.

Heel drop

Flap Heel

A flap heel is easy to do. It is a three-sound step. All you do is add a heel drop after a flap. Start with walking flaps. As you finish each flap, drop your heel. You also can do this step traveling backward.

Flap
Ball Change

Forward brush with your right foot.

Step down with toe of your right foot.

Flap Ball Change

This is a traveling step that has four sounds. Start by doing a flap moving forward on your right foot. Now, with your left foot, do a ball change. When you finish your ball change, your weight should be on your right foot. Your left foot should be free. Now try it on the opposite side.

Shift weight to left foot.

End by shifting weight to your right foot.

MUSICAL FEET

To start making music with your feet, think of a song. Tap it out using simple steps. For example, sing, "Row, Row, Row Your Boat." Clap along as you sing. Clap for every syllable in each word of the song. Now, instead of clapping, use your feet to tap the song. There are many ways you can play this song with your feet. Try this exercise with other songs, too.

CHAPTER FOUR

Beyond Tap Class

There are several ways to build on your love for tap dance. You can attend festivals, competitions, and clubs that focus on tap dance.

Tap Festivals

Tap festivals are good places to learn more about tap dance. A tap festival is a workshop event. Many different classes are offered. The classes are taught by professional tap dancers and choreographers. Tap festivals include performances by master tap dancers and tap dance companies. There also are jam sessions and discussions about tap that students can take part in. Most tap festivals happen in the summer. A few of the larger festivals are held in St. Louis, Missouri; Chicago, Illinois; and New Orleans, Louisiana.

Over 6,000 dancers gather to dance at Tap-O-Mania. Tap-O-Mania is an event held each year on 34th Street in New York City.

39

Competitions

At some point, you may want to compete against other tap dancers. Dance competitions are helpful in developing your tap skills. They make you work harder. Most competitions use a point system to judge each dance routine. There are gold, silver, and bronze rankings. Dancers are judged on their performances. They are judged on technique, style, personality, and appearance. Many local studios select a few dancers to represent them in competitions. Usually dancers have to audition to take part in competitions.

Tap Jams and Jazz Clubs

A tap jam is an event in which tap dancers take turns improvising. To take part, you need some experience improvising. Knowing jazz music is important, too. A good way to practice is to get together with friends. You can take turns improvising steps to your favorite music. You can trade ideas and practice "making conversations" with your feet. You can learn a lot about improvisation by watching experienced dancers in action. Even if you are a beginner, you can benefit from participating in a jam.

Remember, the more you practice tap dance, the better you will become. Who knows? One day you might find yourself tap dancing for an audience.

NEW WORDS

across the floor a part of tap class that focuses on moving dancers across the floor using a combination of steps

ball change a "rocking" step that has two sounds

brush a movement done by striking the ball of the foot on the floor with a kicking motion

choreography the arrangement of tap dance steps

combination several different basic steps that come together to make a more complex step

cramp roll a step that has four sounds

flap a movement done by striking the ball of the foot against the floor in a walking motion

NEW WORDS

flap ball change a traveling step that has four sounds

flap heel same as a flap but with a heel drop added at the end

heel dig a step where the dancer, standing on one leg, strikes the floor with the edge of his or her heel tap

heel drop a forceful dropping of the heel

improvisation tapping without a set routine

rhythm a series of notes or beats that are different in length and stresses

shuffle a two-sound step made up of a forward and backward brush

shuffle ball change same as a shuffle but with a ball change added

tap jam an event where tap dancers take turns improvising tap routines as soloists or in groups

NEW WORDS

taps metal pieces that are attached to the toes and heels of tap shoes to create tapping sounds

toe drop a forceful dropping of the toe

toe punch a movement done by standing on one foot, with the other foot pointed downward, striking the floor with the edge of the toe tap

vaudeville entertainment from the beginning of the 1900s, with comic routines, skits, singing, and dancing

warm-up exercises at the beginning of tap class that loosen up a dancer's muscles

FOR FURTHER READING

Books

Glover, Savion. *Savion!*. New York, NY: William Morrow & Company, Incorporated, 2000.

Knowles, Mark. *The Tap Dance Dictionary*. Jefferson, NC: McFarland & Company, Incorporated Publishers, 1998.

Maurer, Tracy. *Tap Dancing*. Vero Beach, FL: Rourke Press, Incorporated, 1997.

Ormonde, Jimmy. *Tap Dancing at a Glance*. Bedford, MA: Applewood Books, 1996.

RESOURCES

International Tap Association
P.O. Box 356, Boulder, CO 80306
Phone: (303)443-7989

Tap Dance Homepage
www.tapdance.org
This Web site features links to numerous sites dealing with tap schools, equipment, books and videos, and famous tap dancers.

Dance Magazine
www.dancemagazine.com
See the latest issue of *Dance Magazine*. Read article excerpts and columns written by professional choreographers and dancers.

INDEX

INDEX

About the Author

Susan Hebach is a tap dancer, choreographer, and teacher based in New York City. She currently enjoys directing the dance company The Tap Collective, and Tap Dance for Young People, a dance program for children. Ms. Hebach has taught at national conventions throughout the United States. She also has been a visiting faculty in residence at the School of American Dance and Arts Management at Oklahoma City University.